You Are Loved

By: Carrie J. Staten & Louisa J. Staten

Illustrated by: Carrie J. Staten

Dedicated to:

All the L's,

Levi, Lincoln, Louisa, Landry,

Lottie, & Ledrick

You are smart......

.....like a soft snow owl.

You are special...

.....like a sweet panda bear.

You are kind......

.....like a kitten with no scowl.

You are important.....

......like a bee in the air.

You are loved......

......like a dog young or old.

You are funny.....

.....like a furry little llama.

You are brave.....

.....like a lion so bold.

You are clever......

.....like a lizard changing color.

You are obedient......

.....like a seal in the sea.

You are gentle......

...like an elephant so giant.

All of these things
and more......

......you are to me.

And...

.....don't ever forget it.

Made in the USA
San Bernardino, CA
28 October 2018